The Mask of Power

Cynder
Confronts the
Weather Wizard

GROSSET & DUNLAP
Published by the Penguin Group
Penguin Group (USA) LLC, 375 Hudson Street, New York, New York 10014, USA

USA | Canada | UK | Ireland | Australia | New Zealand | India | South Africa | China

penguin.com
A Penguin Random House Company

Written by Cavan Scott
Illustrated by Dani Geremia—Beehive Illustration Agency

ISBN 978-0-448-48718-2   10 9 8 7 6 5 4 3 2 1

The Mask of Power

Cynder
Confronts the
Weather Wizard

by Onk Beakman

Grosset & Dunlap
An Imprint of Penguin Group (USA) LLC

About the Author

Onk Beakman knew he wanted to be a world-famous author from the moment he was hatched. In fact, the book-loving penguin was so excited that he wrote his first novel while still inside his egg (to this day, nobody is entirely sure where he got the tiny pencil and notebook from).

Growing up on the icy wastes of Skylands' Frozen Desert was difficult for a penguin who hated the cold. While his brothers plunged into the freezing waters, Onk could be found with his beak buried in a book and a pen clutched in his flippers.

Yet his life changed forever when a giant floating head appeared in the skies above the tundra. It was Kaos, attempting to melt the icecaps so he could get his grubby little hands on an ancient weapon buried beneath the snow.

Onk watched open-beaked as Spyro swept in and sent the evil Portal Master packing. From that day, Onk knew that he must chronicle the Skylanders' greatest adventures. He traveled the length and breadth of Skylands, collecting every tale he could find about Master Eon's brave champions.

Today, Onk writes from a shack on the beautiful sands of Blistering Beach with his two pet sea cucumbers.

Chapter One

The Oncoming Storm

"Oh yeah," said Zook, reaching for another coconut drink. "This is the life, right, Cynder?"

Beside the Bambazooker, the dark purple dragon shifted uncomfortably beneath the shade of a large umbrella.

"Speak for yourself, Bamboo Boy," she said with a sigh. "Remind me again why we're lying on a beach?"

"To soak up the sun, why else?" The green-barked Life Skylander slurped the creamy coconut milk noisily. "This is the Cloudless Desert, the sunniest spot in all of Skylands.

Just kick back and relax, that's all."

"And you don't feel guilty that we're wasting our time when we should be out looking for the next segment of the Mask of Power?" Cynder snapped, her scaly brow furrowing. She glanced around, taking in the countless Mabu out enjoying a day in the sun. Didn't they realize the danger they were all in? Kaos was trying to reassemble the fabled Mask of Power. If he managed it . . .

"Hey, hey, hey, just chill," insisted Zook, settling back in his deck chair. "If Master Eon needs us, he knows where to find us."

The buzz of the happy vacationers was broken by a sharp crack that sounded like the universe being pulled in two. Cynder was immediately on her feet. She knew that sound. It was a Portal!

She spun around to see a column of light blaze into existence. A figure materialized at its heart. It was tall, regal, and more than a little spooky.

Cynder grinned. Zook wanted to chill and you couldn't get more chilling than this new arrival: Hex!

The elven sorceress swept from the Portal, her piercing gaze passing over the beach. All around, there were gasps and even a few whimpers. Like Cynder, Hex was an Undead Skylander—a mistress of dark magic and feared by many. Hex's ghost-white eyes shimmered as she watched the vacationers frantically pack up their towels and beach chairs, deciding that there was something else they'd rather be doing. Like getting trapped in a spider-infested cave or fed to a pack of zombies.

"What's up, Hexy?" called Zook in greeting. "You here to catch the rays?" The Bambazooker peeked over his pair of ridiculously large sunglasses. "You do look like you could use a tan."

Hex's narrow mouth turned down at the corners. She wasn't known for her sense of humor. She was known for striking fear into everyone's hearts, which was quite different.

"Master Eon needs you," she replied, her voice like wind whistling through a graveyard. "You'll have to 'catch the rays' another time." Her disgust at the very concept was obvious. Hex was more at home in moonlight than in the warmth of the sun.

"Is it the mask?" Cynder said eagerly, feeling an electric thrill run through her wings. "Has Eon located the next segment?"

But Hex didn't answer. Instead she peered into the sky, a puzzled look on her ashen face.

"I thought this place was known as the Cloudless Desert?" she commented, floating up from the blisteringly hot sands.

"Yeah, that's right," Zook confirmed contentedly. "Not a cloud in the sky."

"Except that one," Hex muttered, cocking her head to the side in curiosity.

Cynder followed the witch's gaze. She was right. A tiny cloud had appeared in the expanse of brilliant blue. A cloud that was growing, and growing fast. A shadow fell over the sands as the three Skylanders gazed up in amazement. In a matter of seconds the cloud had smothered the sky, becoming darker with every passing minute.

"Hey, who turned off the sun?" complained Zook, throwing aside his shades and snatching up his bazooka. Fun-loving and carefree he may have been, but

Zook recognized a threat when he saw one.

So did Cynder. Her expression was darkening as quickly as the sky. This was no natural storm.

"It is the power of Darkness," cried Hex. She threw her arms out wide, and crackling phantom orbs appeared in her upturned palms. "The forces of nature have turned against us."

Cynder felt a drop of rain on her nose, followed by another. A moment later, the heavens opened, and water lashed down from those strange storm clouds.

"It could just be a quick shower," joked Zook, ever the eternal optimist. "I mean, who ever got hurt by a few drops of rain?"

There was a scream from their left. The Skylanders turned to see a Mabu sinking into the soggy sand. He was already up to his waist in the quagmire. All around, fleeing vacationers were getting stuck, before getting dragged beneath the dunes.

Cynder could feel the grip of the wet ground pulling her claws down into a clammy embrace.

"We need to do something," she yelled, flapping her leathery wings to pull herself free with a wet squelch. "The dunes are turning into quicksand. Everyone is going to be sucked underground!"

Chapter Two

Quicksand

Cynder soared through the air, snatching a sun-worshipping Mabu from the cloying quicksand and flying him to safety. The rain beat down on her wings the whole time, making it difficult to fly. She wouldn't be able to rescue them all.

"Zook!" she cried out, spotting another Mabu—who was wearing a flowery sunhat—almost vanishing beneath the surface. "Behind you!"

The Bambazooker turned, his eyes growing wide when he spotted the stricken Mabu. "Hang on, little buddy," he shouted out as he splashed through the quagmire.

"T-to what?" stammered the horrified tourist.

"To these!" Zook clapped his hands together and bamboo shoots erupted around the sinking Mabu from beneath the sand. Usually, Zook used his foliage barriers for protection—today they would be a lifeline.

"Great idea, Zook," Cynder called down. "Can you summon them all over the beach?"

"No problem," the Bambazooker yelled back, spinning in a circle. "Let's Zook it up!"

Bamboo shoots popped up here, there, and everywhere.

"Grab hold of the bamboo," Cynder yelled to the Mabu who were still floundering in the mud. "And hang on to them until I can get to you."

"The rain is getting worse," Zook pointed out. "I'm not sure how long the bamboo will last."

"Long enough," murmured Hex, rising up into the air, sinister wreaths of emerald smoke swirling around her hands.

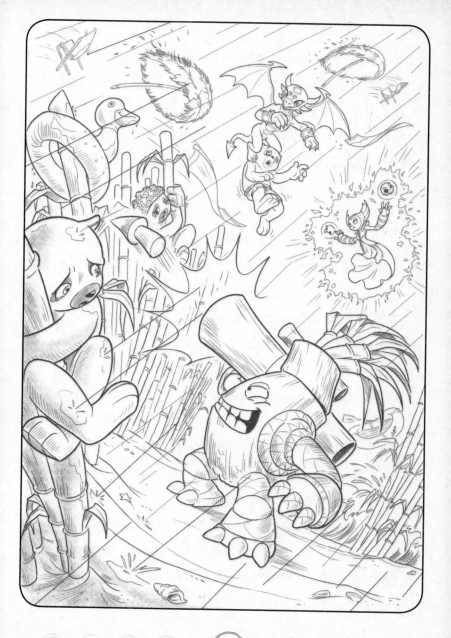

"For what?" Zook asked.

"For the Darkness to fall!" Hex cried out, reaching her hands up to the heavens. Smoke bloomed from her open palms, shooting into the clouds above as the elven witch recited a spell in a language not spoken for thousands upon thousands of years. There was a loud CRACK, and the sky flashed a brilliant green. Even Cynder had to look away from the sudden unnatural flare.

When the dragon looked again the clouds were scuttling away like giant, fluffy spiders.

"Hey, hows about that?" Zook laughed. "Instant summer. Heh-heh!"

Sure enough, beams of sunlight were poking through the retreating clouds, the rain clearing away to nothing.

Not that heros had time to bask in the sun. "Quick, everyone," Cynder snapped, snatching a Mabu out of the drying dunes. "Get clear of the sand before it gets baked hard by the heat. You don't want to get stuck."

Zook joined in, helping to remove the cheering vacationers from the gloopy mess. But when Hex swept down and offered a helping hand, the Mabu recoiled.

"I-it's o-o-okay," one terrified sun-worshipper stammered. "We're f-f-f-fine. In fact, we like it in here."

"Yeah," agreed another struggling vacationer. "B-besides, mud packs are good for the complexion."

Hex's glowing eyes narrowed to slits. She turned, folded her arms across her chest, and stared up at the sun.

"That was some freaky weather," commented Zook, helping the last Mabu out of the sand. "It never rains here."

"Nor should it," pointed out Hex, grimly. "That storm was as natural as me."

"Natural?" laughed a passing sludge-covered Mabu to his companion. "Who's she trying to kid?"

Exactly, Hex hissed to herself, sweeping back to where she had Portalled in.

Cynder slammed down in front of the two giggling Mabus, who soon decided whimpering was a better option.

"You got something to say?" she snarled, spitting out electric blue lightning.

"Nope." The first Mabu gulped.

"Not us," the other said, frantically pulling his big-mouthed buddy in the opposite direction.

"Good. Keep it that way." She glanced up at Hex, who was standing with her head held high. Cynder knew what it was like to be feared. Before seeing the error of her ways, she herself had indulged the darker side of her personality, terrorizing her homeland. But Spyro had shown her that there was a better way. It was different for Hex. She hadn't chosen to become one of the Undead. She had been cursed while protecting innocent souls from evil. And this was how she was repaid.

"I guess we'd better get back to Master Eon," Zook said from behind Cynder, snapping her out of her dark thoughts. "He'll want to know about all this. Hey, you don't think it's got something to do with that Mask of Power thingy, do you?"

"How am I supposed to know?" Cynder snapped, her mind still on Hex. "But I wouldn't be surprised."

Zook just chuckled as he threw his bazooka over his shoulder and wandered after the moody dragon. Undead Skylanders, he thought to himself. Why always so gloomy? They needed to be more like him. What was the point of worrying, anyway?

Chapter Three

A Cry for Help

"Hmmmmm, that is a worry," Master Eon said, rubbing his beard thoughtfully. "Weird weather reports are coming in from all over Skylands. Earlier today, a heatwave hit the Snowcone Mountains."

"Yes," cut in Hugo, Eon's right-hand Mabu. "And the Popcorn Volcano has been covered in fifteen feet of snow. Not to mention what happened back at your citadel, Master Eon."

"At the citadel?" Cynder asked in disbelief. Master Eon's home was usually one of the safest places in Skylands.

"A hailstorm," Hugo replied, wiping his glasses on an oversized hanky. "Hailstones as big as your fist."

"What's so unusual 'bout that?" asked Zook, shrugging at Cynder.

"It hailed *inside* the citadel," Eon answered, his face grave.

"I was taking a bath!" Hugo added, with a sniffle. "I've never been so scared in my life."

"Could be worse," said Cynder slyly.

"How?" asked the Mabu, already looking nervous.

"It could have been raining sheep!" the dragon replied, grinning wickedly. The Skylanders were always teasing Hugo about his bizarre fear of ewes and lambs. Sure enough, the little historian began to panic.

"Is that possible, Master Eon?" he asked in alarm, clutching the Portal Master's robes. "Can we expect a deluge of those scheming woolly devils?"

"I sincerely doubt it, Hugo," Eon said,

fixing Cynder with a stare. "And this is no laughing matter."

"Indeed," agreed Hex, whose mood hadn't improved—although it was difficult to tell thanks to the constant scowl on her face. "It is as if the elements are revolting."

"Well, that rain certainly was," Zook quipped cheerfully, sighing when no one laughed. "At least everything's A-OK here at the archive."

Cynder wasn't so sure. While they searched for the fragments of the Mask of Power, Eon and the Skylanders had temporarily switched their base to the Eternal Archive, home to both the Warrior Librarians and the infamous Book of Power and Other Utterly Terrifying Stuff (Vol. 3). This enchanted tome was gradually revealing the locations of the eight segments of the Mask that had been scattered across Skylands thousands of years ago. The book had been protected by the librarians for generations.

On the surface, the librarians looked like

your average, run-of-the-mill, gigantic robots, but beneath each one's metallic armor sat a tiny bookworm who was piloting the fierce-looking suit. They'd gathered every book in the known universe and guarded each one jealously within the walls of their imposing archive.

Cynder had taken an instant dislike to the place. It was too quiet. Usually, the only sound you could hear was the Warrior Librarians telling people to *shhh*. Of course, she knew that was normal for libraries, but in other libraries the librarians weren't likely to try to take your head off if you kept talking. Take Squirmgrub, the librarian who had been assigned to help them with the Book of Power. Even now, standing at a respectful distance, the armored archivist had a sword clasped in his metal fist. No wonder people were scared of being overdue with a book. Luckily, Master Eon and the chief curator were old friends. But, as far as Cynder was concerned, the sooner they were out of here the better.

"Do you think these bizarre weather

conditions are linked to what's happening on the Isle of the Undead, Master Eon?" asked Hugo, still trembling at the thought of a shower of sinister sheep.

Cynder's ears pricked up. "The Isle of the Undead? What's that got to do with anything?"

"I'm not sure," Eon admitted. "We received a call for help from the island dwellers this morning."

"But they hate outsiders," said Hex, who was as intrigued as Cynder. "No Skylander has set foot on the island for five hundred years."

Hex wasn't joking. The Isle of the Undead was a dark and forbidding island set in the middle of a dark and forbidding sea that was surrounded by even darker and more forbidding mountains. It was said to be the place where bad dreams were born, where even monsters feared to tread. Which was exactly why Cynder had always wanted to go there.

"The plea came from the Night Mayor himself—Morbo the Macabre," explained

Hugo, shivering at the very mention of the name. "The message was written on bat-wing leather, using bloodred spiderling webbing. Ugh!"

"So what's the problem?" asked Zook, looking eager to get going. Unlike the rest of his tribe, the Bambazooker lived to explore—oh, and to blast things with his bazooka, of course.

"That's the strange thing," said Eon. "The message simply read, 'Please send help.' Nothing more, nothing less."

Cynder frowned. "Could it be a trap?"

"I'm not sure," Eon admitted. "And then there's the small matter of what the Book of Power showed me this morning."

Squirmgrub's head shot up. "Th-the Book of Power?" the Warrior Librarian said, his mechanical voice unnaturally shrill. "You didn't tell me you were going down to the Forbidden Vault."

"No," said Eon tersely, not looking at Squirmgrub. "I did not." Cynder glanced over at the towering librarian. Like many of the Skylanders, Cynder thought there was something not quite right about this particular archivist. Was Master Eon getting just as suspicious?

"And what did you find?" asked Hex, floating nearer.

Eon reached into one of his sleeves and pulled out a scroll of parchment.

"The book showed me a map," he said, unrolling the paper.

"The location of the Life segment?" Hugo asked, wringing his hands together.

"I'm not sure," Eon admitted. "But I took the liberty of making a copy just in case."

"But a map of what?" demanded Squirmgrub, surprisingly brusquely.

Eon turned the paper toward them, showing a perfect drawing of a storm-battered island, located in the middle of a black sea and surrounded by a looming range of jagged mountains.

"The Isle of the Undead." Cynder gasped.

Chapter Four

The Isle of the Undead

"Bamboo-yaaaaaaa-ARGH!" Zook yelled as he jumped from Master Eon's Portal. Hex had warned him that the island was a dark and stormy place, but he hadn't expected to be hit by lightning the moment he arrived. "Woah," he said, shaking his trunk to clear his head. "That's one shocking welcome."

"What did you expect?" Cynder snickered, appearing beside him. "This is the Isle of the Undead."

"One of the spookiest and deadliest places in Skylands," added Hex as she materialized behind the others, warily eyeing up Zook.

Normally, any living soul who set foot in an Undead realm would instantly join the legions of the Undead. But, like all Skylanders, Zook was protected from the Isle of the Undead's dark power by one of Eon's spells. Still, Hex couldn't resist peering at Zook to make sure all was as it should be. Satisfied, she floated forward to check if the coast was clear. "Stay on your guard," she continued. "There are creatures here that would startle even the strongest heart. Hideous beasts and foul spirits lurk at every turn."

"Yeah," grinned Cynder. "Isn't it great?"

"If you like gloomy and grim forests, I guess." Zook looked around at the gnarled old trees that stretched up to the glowering sky. His leaves were still smoldering from the lightning strike. "But hey, it's new. I like new. What are we waiting for? Let's find this Morbo guy."

"And the Undead segment of the mask, too," reminded Cynder. "Surely it's no coincidence that we've been summoned to the exact same place the book displayed?"

"Wait!" Hex interrupted, floating in front of them. "We are not alone!"

"We're not?" asked Zook, his grin fading ever so slightly as he swung his bazooka into firing position.

"No, I sense something is watching us. Something evil."

Cynder spun around. She couldn't see anything.

"There's nothing here!" she whispered, her scales tingling with anticipation.

"Yeah, there is," said Zook. "Heads up!"

Cynder looked up, straight into the many eyes of a gigantic Gargantula!

The monstrous spider dropped from its web, sticky saliva spraying from its snapping jaws. Its six muscular, hairy legs were raised, ready to crash down on Cynder. "Volts and lightning!" she exclaimed, opening her mouth to unleash a blast of black bolts. While some dragons breathed fire,

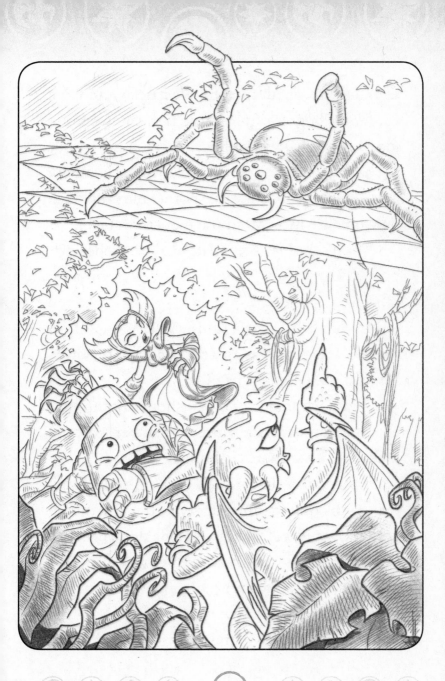

Cynder breathed spectral electricity, and the Gargantula got a full charge right between its many eyes. It shrieked as it was knocked out of the way, landing on its massive back, all six legs scrabbling in the air. Another blast of black lightning disintegrated the monster forever.

"Ha! That was a blast!" Cynder cheered.

"So are they," warned Zook, pointing forward. "Look out!"

Cynder looked again. A legion of tiny yellow arachnids was scuttling from where the Gargantula had been.

"Spiderlings!" Cynder shouted, zapping the four-legged creatures with her electric breath. "Now that's just cheating."

"Do not let them touch you," Hex advised, firing orbs of uncanny energy at the advancing carpet of spiders. "They explode on contact."

"That might be trickier than you'd think," shouted Zook, aiming his bazooka at the trees. "They're everywhere."

Zook was right. Spiderlings were crawling

down every single tree. The Bambazooker was firing shell after shell into the swarm, but it wasn't doing any good. For every Spiderling he blasted, half a dozen took its place.

"Stand back-to-back," Hex ordered. "Cover every angle."

"They'll be covering us in a minute, heh-heh," Zook pointed out as they fell into position.

"Not if they can't get to us," Hex disagreed, clapping her hands together. A ring of giant bones burst out of the ground, surrounding them. "My Bone Fortress has held back Cyclops Mammoths and Skull Golems."

"A few hundred Spiderlings shouldn't be a problem then." Zook grinned, ever the optimist.

"Not unless they're small enough to crawl through your rack of ribs," pointed out Cynder, ever the pessimist. Sure enough, Spiderling legs were already appearing around the tightly packed bones.

"No worries. Old Zook'll fill in the gaps," said Zook, preparing to summon a ring of bamboo to bolster Hex's bones.

SPLUT!

Something sticky hit him on the shoulder.

"Uh-oh," he said. "Spider webbing."

Zook was pulled off his feet and yanked through Hex's bony defences toward the Gargantula that was reeling him in. If this wasn't bad enough, every time he bounced over a Spiderling, it exploded beneath him.

"Ow! Ow! Ow!"

"No rest for the wicked." Cynder sighed, flying out of the bone circle. She came about, her mouth open, ready to blast the Gargantula that was about to snack on Zook.

THWACK!

Cynder cried out as she flew headfirst into something—something she couldn't see.

"What is this?" she yelled as she thrashed around, only succeeding in becoming more entangled in her invisible restraints.

"Stop struggling," Hex commanded from below, now trying to hold back the Spiderlings by herself.

"Easy for you to say."

"You're trapped in a Moon Widow's web," Hex shouted. "The stickiest threads of all. The more you fight, the worse it will become."

Cynder forced herself to be still. Hex was right. She had flown straight into a huge web, the strands so thin they could hardly be seen, yet still as strong as steel. Above her, a bloated four-legged spider was descending. A Moon Widow—as poisonous as her web was tough.

"Hex," Cynder cried out, looking back down at her friend. "Got an anti-spider spell up your sleeve?" But her voice trailed off. Hex was still in the middle of the bone circle but something had changed. There was a tree in there beside her. An old dead tree. And it hadn't been there before.

Cynder's eyes widened as she realized what it was. "Hex, look out," she bellowed in warning. "Stump Demon!"

But it was too late. With the sound of splintering wood, long, twisted arms burst out of the tree trunk, the bark splitting open to reveal two glaring eyes and a mouth full of sharp wooden teeth. With a roar, the Stump Demon lunged at Hex.

Chapter Five

The Stump Demon

"No!" Cynder roared as the Stump Demon attacked, its clawed hand rushing down to strike Hex.

Or so Cynder had thought. At the last minute, the demonic tree twisted, its massive fist smashing into the ground. Roots shot out in every direction like the spokes of a gnarled wooden wheel, ripping through the soil and hitting the advancing Spiderlings. The scuttling yellow bundles detonated, triggering a chain reaction that wiped out the whole swarm.

The creature lurched back at Hex, who

immediately threw up her hands to defend herself with a spell.

"No!" shouted a voice from amid the Stump Demon's twisted branches. A translucent head appeared. It was a ghost wearing a huge pair of glasses.

"Help your friends," the specter shouted. "We'll hold back as many spiders as we can."

Hex spun in place, reciting an ancient spell. There was a crack of thunder above and it began to rain—not water, but screaming, glowing skulls. They fell on the Moon Widow's web, their chattering teeth chomping through the strands with ease. Cynder tumbled back to the forest floor, flapped her wings, and flipped over, landing next to Zook's bazooka.

"Missing this?" With a whack of her tail, Cynder sent the weapon skittering across to Zook. The Bambazooker grabbed his boom-tube and aimed it into the Gargantula's bulging belly.

"Locked and loaded," he grinned, pulling the trigger.

BANG!

The giant spider was sent spiralling back into the trees, but Zook didn't celebrate. Instead he twisted, pointing the bazooka straight at Cynder!

"Hey, what are you—?"

Zook fired. The hardwood shell rocketed straight over Cynder's head and smashed into the Moon Widow that had reared up behind her. With a startled shriek, the four-legged beastie scuttled away to safety.

"Woah," Cynder said, puffing her cheeks out in relief. "Thanks, Zook."

"No prob—," smiled the ever-cheerful Skylander, wiping sticky spider spit from his arm. "We beat them bad."

"Thanks to our new friends," reminded Hex as she banished her bone fortress with a snap of her fingers. The bones crumbled into dust to reveal the Stump Demon, who instantly roared and raised its huge arms to swipe at the sorceress.

"You sure it's friendly?" asked Zook, preparing to fire at the creature.

"He is, he is," said the ghost with the gigantic glasses, popping out again from the Stump Demon's branches.

"Really?" said Cynder, stalking forward. She wasn't quite ready to trust a Stump Demon just yet.

"Well, no. The truth of the matter is that he's a ravenous monster who is the enemy of all living beings," admitted the ghost. "But he's promised the mayor that he'll help you. We both have."

"That must go against the grain," Cynder sneered. "A Stump Demon forced turn over a new leaf."

The Stump Demon growled ominously.

"And the tree puns aren't helping, trust me," the ghost cut in, placing a placating, soothing hand on the Stump Demon's trunk.

"There there, Dogwood. Good boy. They don't mean anything by it."

Dogwood didn't look like he believed the bespectacled specter. In fact, he looked as if he was considering biting the ghost's hand clean off.

"And you are?" asked Zook, finally dropping his bazooka.

"My name is Flunky," the ghost replied, bowing slightly. "The Night Mayor's personal secretary."

"Well, whoever you two are," Cynder said, never taking her eyes off the Stump Demon, "you arrived just in time. We nearly became spider snacks."

"What she means to say is *thank you!*" Zook chuckled.

Flunky waved the gratitude away. "Don't mention it. The Night Mayor sent us to meet you. We're to take you to him."

"Why did Morbo call for us?" Hex asked.

"I'm sure he will explain," replied Flunky, indicating for them to follow him. "I just hope you can get to the root of our problem."

"Heh-heh!" guffawed Zook, as Dogwood roared with displeasure. "Now who's making tree puns?"

Flunky looked worriedly at the Stump Demon. "I didn't mean it like that. You know that, don't you, Dogwood, old pal, old chum?" The Stump Demon just glared at the ghost, who nervously led the Skylanders deeper into the forest.

Night Mayor Morbo was possibly the plumpest ghost that Cynder had ever seen. He was standing—or should that be floating?—in the middle of Ghost Town, the capital of the Isle of the Undead. A cobweb-covered top hat was perched on his transparent head, and a huge chain of golden bones hung around his spectral neck.

As the Skylanders walked into the town square, led by Flunky and Dogwood, Cynder could feel hundreds of spectral eyes resting on them. It was clear that no one had seen a living soul here for a very long time.

"Skylanders," the mayor exclaimed as he spotted them, his voice sounding like a whisper on the wind. "How horrible to see you."

"Eh?" said Zook, confused. "I thought he invited us."

"It's just how they talk here," Hex whispered, trying not to cause offense. "Horrible means . . ." She searched for the right word. When she found it, the look on her face told Zook that it wasn't one she often used. "It means delightful. Foul means fair. Fair means foul."

"You'll soon get used to it," said Cynder.

"Good," said Zook. "Or do I mean bad?"

"I understand you were attacked by some of our six-legged friends on your arrival," Morbo murmured. "How utterly lovely for you. Please accept my apologies. I have put the word out that you are not to be harmed."

"You are most kind," Hex said, bowing in gratitude.

"And you are the most disgusting creature I have ever seen," the mayor simpered, gazing lovingly at the sorceress.

"Hey, there's no need to be rude," Zook cut in, trigger finger itching.

"He's not," hissed Cynder quickly. "Remember? Bad is good."

"Disgusting is beautiful?" Zook asked, scratching his leaves.

"You'll get it soon," Cynder insisted, before turning her attention back to the ghost. "So, Mayor Morbo. How can we help?"

The mayor checked the watch that hung from his golden chain of bones and his face fell.

"I'm afraid you're about to find out."

Chapter Six

Hurrikazam

The clock struck thirteen. Suddenly, without warning, the dark clouds that usually rolled across the island's leaden sky vanished, and beams of bright sunlight shone down.

"Woah!" exclaimed Zook. "Where are my shades when I need them?"

Beside him, Mayor Morbo stifled a sob. "See? This is the problem. No one has ever needed sunglasses on the Isle of the Undead before."

"But this is impossible." Cynder gasped as the sun immediately warmed her scales.

"It's never daytime on the Isle of the Undead!"

"Someone tell that to the sun!" Zook said, grinning from ear to ear. "It's beautiful."

"Exactly. It's the best thing that has ever happened to us!" moaned the mayor, meaning the complete opposite, of course.

All around them, green shoots sprouted from the cracked earth, leaves immediately unfurling on usually dead branches. Blossoms were even appearing on Dogwood's arms.

"Awwwww, no. Not again. Pretty flowers. That's all I need."

"I can see why you sent for us," Hex said in hushed tones. "This much beauty and life must be agony for you all."

"Yeah," Cynder agreed. "The Isle of the Undead is known for its dark and stormy nights, not its bright and breezy days."

"And the worst is yet to come," Morbo said, pointing into the sky. "Look."

The Skylanders followed his gaze. A cloud had formed, but not like the one that had caused so much trouble in the Cloudless Desert. Yes, this cloud was growing in size as it approached the island, but that wasn't all. The cloud was changing shape. The nearer it got, the more it looked like a gigantic head.

Zook's bazooka already had the fluffy cloud in his sights. "Heads up!" he shouted. "Literally. You thinking what I'm thinking?"

Cynder bared her fangs. "If you're thinking that a huge head in the sky usually means only one thing, then yeah. I sure am."

"Kaos," Hex hissed, orbs rising from her open palms. "Prepare to rest in peace, foul follower of Darkness."

"Rest in peace?" Zook laughed. "He'll rest in *pieces* when I'm finished with him. Heh-heh."

But Cynder wasn't so sure. She was peering at the cloud that had grown to fifty times its original size and was now hanging directly over the town. "Wait up, guys. That doesn't look like Kaos."

Zook squinted, looking closer at the cloud.

"I don't know. It's ugly enough to be Kaos."

"I'll give you that, bamboo boy," Cynder admitted. "But since when did Kaos have long white hair?"

"And an even longer mustache," Hex added, still ready for action.

Sure enough, the giant head had flowing silver locks that waved in the breeze and a thick, silky mustache hanging down underneath its massive hooked nose. As they watched, the cloud shifted again to form a gigantic pointed hat, festooned with lightning bolts and suns.

"No, that isn't Kaos," confirmed Morbo, as the cloud's shadow settled over the town square. "It's someone much, much worse."

"Worse than Kaos?" repeated Zook. "Is that even possible?"

"Silence," boomed the head, its voice like seventeen thunderstorms rolled into one. "The Mighty Hurrikazam demands your tribute."

"Demands our what?" Cynder asked, her ears still ringing.

"Our tribute," said Morbo sadly. "An offering. It's the same every day. Flunky, tell them to bring forth the tribute."

"Yes, Mr. Mayor. Right away," Flunky said, hurrying over to the town hall. "What are you waiting for? Bring out the pies!"

Zook's eyes lit up. "Batterson's pies? Mmm-mmmm. Is it lunchtime already?"

"Only for him," grumbled Morbo.

Cynder turned to see a parade of ghosts and zombies streaming out of the town hall, each carrying a huge, steaming pie. The smell was mouthwatering. Zook had been right. These were Batterson's pies. They were the tastiest, juiciest, most delicious pies in all of Skylands—and, bizarrely, the Undead's favorite delicacy.

Of course, it hadn't always been like this. For centuries, the Undead had terrorized the living, pouring out of their tombs to cause havoc.

But that all changed when an enterprising Molekin baker by the name of Batterson opened a bakery in Darklight Crypt. The ghouls went gaga for Batterson's pastries and gave up haunting on the spot. Why spend all your time freaking out mortals when you could be feasting on succulent pastry morsels instead? Now Batterson's pie shops were springing up all over Skylands and were loved by both the living and the Undead—and, it seemed, Hurrikazam.

"Bring me my pies," the huge head demanded, its fluffy mouth visibly watering. "Bring them to me NOOOOOW!"

As the head howled the last word, a dark twisting vortex appeared beside the cloud. Mini tornadoes spilled from the rift in the sky and spun down toward the parading pie-bearers. One by one, the tiny twisters plucked the island dwellers from the ground and lifted them spinning back up toward Hurrikazam, pies and all.

"He's ghost-napping them," Cynder cried out in alarm as the first tornado buzzed

back beneath the head's monstrous mustache. "We've got to stop him."

Cynder leaped forward, grabbing the foot of a ghost that had already been whipped up into a whirlwind. The spook's pie spun out of its hands as Cynder pulled it loose and landed with a *plop* on the ground.

"Oh no," wailed Morbo. "The crust has broken! We are doomed!"

"Don't worry," said Flunky, attempting to scoop the pastry back into the pie dish. "It's not that bad! Wooooooah!"

Another tornado had whizzed down and snatched up the spectral private secretary. Beneath him, Dogwood roared in anger and reached up in an attempt to grab Flunky, but he too was snatched up by the mini storm. Stump Demon and bespectacled ghost alike spun through the air toward Hurrikazam.

"Let him go!" Cynder roared into the whirlwind-filled air. Beside her, Zook swung his bazooka up on to his shoulder.

"Don't sweat it," he said. "This big head will soon be shell-shocked."

Chuckling to himself, Zook squinted down his bazooka's sights and squeezed his trigger. Hurrikazam was about to get blasted right between his cloudy white eyes.

Chapter Seven

Lightning Strike

"No!" shouted Morbo, barging into Zook. The Bambazooker fired, but his shot went wild, soaring harmlessly into the sky.

"What are you doing?" Zook yelled, struggling to bring his bamboo-tube back to point at Hurrikazam. "I could have stopped him!"

"We can't," Morbo whined, keeping a meaty hand on the bazooka. "Hurrikazam is the most powerful Weather Wizard we've ever seen. If we don't meet his demands—"

"He won't restore the bad weather,"

Hex said solemnly, finishing the Night Mayor's sentence.

Above them, the last of the tornadoes were spinning into the Weather Wizard's vortex.

"Exactly," Morbo said, looking crestfallen. "It's the only way."

High in the sky, the Weather Wizard's vortex finally closed, a satisfied smirk stretching across his cloudy face.

"It's time this billowing bully was taught a lesson," Cynder declared, launching into the air.

"What have we here?" Hurrikazam bellowed as Cynder sped toward him. "*Tsk.* That's the only problem with picnicking in the sunshine. There are always annoying bugs."

"Sorry to spoil your snack." Cynder sneered, coming level with Hurrikazam's ginormous eyes. "Now, send those specters right back."

"Or what?"

"Or this!" Cynder roared, a sparking stream of spectral lightning bursting from her open mouth. The dark energy slammed straight into Hurrikazam's smirking face.

"Ha!" the Weather Wizard boomed, the electricity arcing up and down his misty mustache. "Think yourself a bright spark, do you?"

Cynder glared. Usually enemies evaporated in a blaze of light when hit by her spectral lightning. At the very least they looked shocked. Hurrikazam was just laughing.

"Using lightning to fight a meteorological mage? Not so bright after all!"

Cynder's jaws snapped shut, exhausted. The Weather Wizard had absorbed everything she had. Time for plan B.

Cynder started to fly around and around in a circle.

"There's no need to get yourself in a tizzy," mocked Hurrikazam.

You'll be laughing on the other side of your cloud, Cynder thought as she pushed herself even faster. Within seconds she was an indigo blur.

Far below, Zook cheered her on. "That's it,

girl," he shouted, waving his bazooka. "Send that selfish storm cloud back where he came from!"

"But what's she doing?" asked Morbo, bewildered at the sight.

"A high-altitude shadow dance," breathed Hex in admiration. "She's summoning a ghost-haunter attack."

"Yeah." Zook giggled. "Old fog-face is going to get more spooks than he can swallow."

Sure enough, glowing ghosts started to manifest themselves in Cynder's wake, an army of apparitions that turned angrily on the Weather Wizard.

Hurrikazam just laughed louder than ever.

"Am I supposed to be scared?" he chortled. "Am I supposed to quake in my boots? If I had boots, I mean."

The Skylanders heard Cynder's defiant reply as the ghosts started streaking toward the cloud. "This day will haunt you forever!" she screamed, more ghouls appearing all around her.

"Ha!" The Weather Wizard barked. "You don't stand a *ghost* of a chance against me. You tried your lightning. Now try mine."

Hex shouted out a warning, but it was too late. Bolts of lightning blazed from Hurrikazam's eyes, lancing through the ghostly guards and zapping into Cynder. The dragoness cried out in surprise and then plummeted to the ground, wings still sparking with Hurrikazam's fiendish electricity.

Chapter Eight

Under the Weather

"Levitate!"

Hex shot into the air and caught Cynder as she fell. Zook, meanwhile, was firing volley after volley of high-velocity shells at the Weather Wizard.

"Please," begged Morbo. "Don't anger him."

"He angered *me*," snapped Zook, his usual happy-go-lucky persona slipping for a second. "How d'ya like that, cloud-chops?"

The shells exploded harmlessly against Hurrikazam's fleecy cheeks.

"Oh, I'm cool with it," he shouted back. "But not as cold as you!"

"What's he talking about," Zook said, his wooden brow furrowing. "I'm not c-c-c-cold."

"Then why are your teeth chattering?" Morbo asked, but Zook couldn't answer. When the Night Mayor looked again, a blanket of sparkling frost had spread over the Bambazooker, freezing him in place.

Above them, Hex was clutching Cynder with one hand and conjuring a spell with the other.

"You will bow down before my power," she growled, orbs spinning from her fingers. "All hail the dark arts."

"Hmmmm," mused Hurrikazam. "'Hail,' you say? What a splendid idea, witch."

The Weather Wizard's face darkened and Hex found herself pummelled by hailstones the size of beach balls. She twisted, shielding the still-stunned Cynder from the onslaught, and was forced back down to the ground.

"I have had my fill of your pies and your insolence," boomed Hurrikazam triumphantly.

"I will return when the clock strikes thirteen tomorrow. And hear this—if you dare defy Hurrikazam again, I will make sure that darkness never returns to your miserable little island. Remember, the Weather Wizard rains supreme!"

With a peal of thunderous laughter, the cloud dissipated and with it the sunshine. The island was plummeted into darkness, the newly grown flowers withering and dying instantly.

"Thank the dark powers." Morbo sighed in relief. "We have survived another day."

"Survived?" Cynder said, still shaking from the lightning attack. "But what about all those ghosts?"

"A-and F-f-f-flunky," shivered a rapidly thawing Zook. "He was s-s-s-snatched too, remember?"

"As if I could forget," Morbo insisted mournfully. "It's the same every day. Hurrikazam appears at the witching hour, demanding that we hand over at least twenty pies. Or else."

"Or else what?" asked Hex, her face grave.

"Or else he'll make the sun shine forever," replied Morbo, wincing at the thought. "An endless summer."

"What's wrong with a little sun, eh?" Zook said, brushing the last of the frost from his arms. "Could give you a tan."

"And destroy their crops," Hex said sharply. "Undead plants need bad weather to grow. Darkness. Storms. Freezing conditions."

"That's right." Morbo nodded. "Nothing would grow in the sun, except for "—he paused, hardly able to say the word—"flowers."

"And that would be bad," said Cynder.

"You mean good," corrected Zook.

"Whatever." Cynder sighed.

"But what about the Island Dwellers he abducts with the pies?" Hex asked. "Do you ever see them again?"

A shadow passed over Morbo's face. "No. They're gone forever. All except . . ." His voice trailed off.

"Except?"

Morbo looked at each Skylander in turn. "Someone did come back, but they had changed beyond all recognition."

"Can we see them?" Cynder asked.

Morbo nodded. "If you must. But prepare yourself. It's enough to give you nightmares—even when you're awake."

"Heh-heh. There sure are a lot of stairs," Zook said with a chuckle as the Skylanders followed Morbo down into the Town Hall's basement.

"F-five flights," Morbo confirmed, stammering with nervousnesses. "We need to k-keep him down here. Away from everyone."

Hex didn't like the sound of that. "In the dark? Is that completely necessary?"

"Oh a-absol-lu-lu-lutley," Morbo replied, his chains clanking together as he trembled. "No one came out of their h-h-houses when we kept him upstairs. B-besides, he was putting me off my t-t-tea . . ."

The lower they descended, the worse the Night Mayor stammered.

"Sheesh," Zook whispered to Cynder. "Morbo looks like he's seen, well, himself."

"This is more serious than we first thought," Hex warned from behind. "There isn't much in Skylands that can scare a ghost."

"So, this Hurrikazam guy?" asked Zook. "He turns night into day, darkness into light?"

Cynder immediately picked up on what he was getting at. "You think he's got something to do with the segment?"

"Using the complete opposite of the Undead Element against the Undead themselves," pondered Hex. "A distinct possibility."

They continued down the staircase, Morbo shuddering as they reached the lower basement. "I-i-it isn't too I-late to ch-ch-change your m-m-mind."

"We'll be fine," Cynder said softly. "Don't worry about us."

"I-I wasn't," admitted the mayor. "I was w-w-worried about me. V-very well, h-here we are."

The spooked spook snapped his fingers, and—as if by magic (which is exactly what it was)—torches blazed into life in the corridor ahead of them. By the flickering light of the flames, the Skylanders could see a solitary door at the end of the passage.

"Are they in there?" Cynder asked, wide-eyed.

Morbo nodded with a whimper. "H-he said he escaped from the wizard's cloud. We f-f-found him hiding behind a tomb in the graveyard. He wouldn't let us s-see him at first. I s-sometimes wish I hadn't p-persuaded him to come out."

"Hey, it can't be that bad," said Zook cheerfully, marching down the corridor. "Trust me, we've seen scary stuff. Monsters. Gorgons. Kaos' feet."

"Y-you don't understand," Morbo said,

floating behind the Skylanders who were already rushing after Zook. "It's like nothing you've ever seen."

Zook had reached the door by now and was reaching for the knob.

"P-p-please reconsider," pleaded Morbo, rushing ahead of them and placing a warning hand on Zook's. "People have gone mad looking at what's in that room."

"Really," snarled Cynder, beginning to lose her temper with the shaky specter. "We'll be fine."

"Okay," said Morbo, gliding aside. "It's your f-f-funeral."

Chuckling at the nervous ghost, Zook turned the handle. The door was stiff, creaking as the Bambazooker pushed it open.

The room inside was pitch black.

"Um, hello?" ventured Zook, stepping into the darkness.

"Hello," returned a weak, wheezing voice.

"There's nothing to be afraid of," Zook

said breezily, fighting the urge to swallow nervously. Even he was getting the jitters. "We're Skylanders and we're here to help."

"Oh, there's *everything* to be afraid of," said the voice from the shadows.

"Hex?" said Cynder, peering into the dark. "Can you help us out with a little light?"

"Gladly," the witch replied, sending a glowing orb up to the ceiling.

The three Skylanders gasped as one as they finally saw what was sitting in the center of the room.

Chapter Nine

The Thing in the Room

"Is that it?" asked a mystified Cynder. "Is that what everyone is so afraid of?"

"Y-y-yes," whimpered Morbo, purposely looking the other way. "Don't say I didn't w-w-warn you."

"But," started an equally confused Zook, "it's just a . . ."

"I-I know."

"Mabu," completed Hex.

The sorceress was right. There, sitting in the middle of the room, illuminated by Hex's orb, was the most lovable Mabu you could ever hope to see.

"Awww," cooed Zook. "He's adorable!"

"Waaaaaaaaaaah!" wailed the Mabu, bursting into tears. "See? I'm adorable."

"You are." Zook nodded enthusiastically. "Real cute."

"Cuuuuute!" The Mabu bawled. "This is the worst day of my un-life!"

"What did I say?" Zook shrugged, looking at his friends in bewilderment.

A look of realization passed over Cynder's scales. "Of course," she said, turning her attention to the snivelling Mabu. "What's your name?"

"Rib Cage," the Mabu sniffed in reply.

"Strange name for a Mabu," Zook commented.

"A strange name indeed," agreed Hex, also realizing what had happened.

"You weren't always a Mabu, were you?" asked Cynder, taking a tentative step forward. The Mabu shook his head.

"What were you?"

"I was a skeleton," Rib Cage howled. "A terrifying, bone-white, Undead skeleton."

Hex swept past Cynder and rushed toward the Mabu.

"And now you're . . ." She paused, not quite believing what she was saying. "Alive?"

"Yes," said Morbo from behind, his voice betraying his disgust. "This is how we found him."

"I was Undead when I got sucked up by one of the Weather Wizard's tornadoes," Rib Cage explained, pulling a tissue out of his pocket. "And now look at me. I'm a freak."

"Even his family has disowned him," Morbo reported with a shake of his head.

"They made no bones about it," sniffed Rib Cage. "Said they wouldn't be seen alive with me."

Cynder frowned. "How did this happen?"

"It was the wizard. That big head isn't really him. It's a floating magical lair—his Cloud Citadel."

"And what's inside?" Hex asked, hanging on to Rib Cage's every word.

"Some kind of factory," Rib Cage remembered, "with plants and flowers everywhere. There are birds and butterflies and the sweetest smells imaginable."

"The complete opposite to the Isle of the Undead," said Cynder quietly, sharing a knowing look with Hex.

"Sounds beautiful," Zook said, smiling at the thought.

"Exactly," said Rib Cage, shuddering at the memory. "We were placed beneath a machine that looked like a big metal cloud. Hurrikazam threw a switch, and it started to rain. Huge, fresh raindrops, drenched us in seconds. And when the rain stopped, I . . ." His voice dissolved into sobs again.

"I-I can't bear it," said Morbo, also fighting back the tears.

"It's okay," comforted Cynder, as gently as she could. "You can tell us."

"When the rain stopped, I was like this," Rib Cage sniffed. "My Undead nature had been washed away. I was alive."

"Can that even happen?" asked Zook, scratching his trunk.

"No," insisted Cynder, shaking her head. "It's impossible."

"But it's true," Morbo said solemnly. "Our local witch doctor has performed every test he knows. Rib Cage is alive. He has a heartbeat and everything."

"But it must be a trick," Cynder said, not knowing what to believe. "No one can bring the Undead to life."

"Why not?" said Hex, her voice as cold as ice. "The living can be made Undead. Why not the other way around?"

"There's something else that doesn't make sense," cut in Zook, eager to change the conversation. "I heard of Hurrikazam on my travels. Everyone said he was a nice guy, one of the best. Wouldn't hurt a fly."

"His lightning didn't feel so kind to me," remembered Cynder.

"Exactly. So what changed, eh? Why start blackmailing an entire island?"

"I don't know," said Cynder, glancing nervously at Hex, who was staring off into the distance, lost in her own thoughts. "But I know how to find out."

Chapter Ten

The Plan

"Are you sure this is a good idea?" Mayor Morbo asked the Skylanders the following day.

"Nope." Zook smiled. "That's why it's fun."

"But you could be putting yourself in terrible danger."

Zook nodded eagerly. "More fun. This is a good day!"

Zook grinned even when he was in grave peril. In fact, the bigger the risk, the more he beamed. It was infectious, and Cynder couldn't help but crack a little smile of her own.

"It's nearly time," Cynder said, forcing

herself to focus on the matter at hand. The last thing she needed was to be seen walking around with a silly smirk on her face. She had a reputation to protect. "Are you sure they'll come?"

"They gave me their word," said Morbo, checking his watch. "They'll be here."

As if they'd heard him, a rustling came from the jagged thornbushes that lined the town square. One by one, three hideous Gargantulas stalked toward the Skylanders.

"Aha! Here they are," declared the Night Mayor, floating forward to address the gigantic six-legged spiders. "Now, remember what we agreed. No biting our guests. Not even a nibble. They're here to help us. Do you understand?"

The Gargantulas nodded, chittering ominously, before turning toward the Skylanders.

"Okay, who's going first?" asked Morbo expectantly.

"Me, me, me!" exploded Zook, jumping up and down on the spot, his arm waving in the air.

"Choose me! Choose me! Choose me!"

"Hex first," said Cynder, unable to resist. (Not that the kickback seemed to worry Zook in the slightest. If anything, it only made him even more eager.)

Hex, on the other hand, said nothing. In fact, she'd hardly spoken since they'd met Rib Cage. She swept forward and turned her back onto the first Gargantula. The monster reared up on its hind legs behind Hex as another spider scuttled around to face her.

Hex didn't even flinch as the spider shot a stream of sticky webbing straight at her. It pushed her back against the hairy belly of the waiting Gargantula and held her fast. The spider twisted its head, spewing more webs. Seconds later, Hex couldn't move. She was stuck to the Gargantula's stomach like glue.

"Okay, let's see what it looks like," ordered Cynder. The Gargantula dropped back to four feet, Hex beneath its body.

"Can you see me?" Hex asked from beneath the spider.

Cynder smiled. "Not at all. The plan is going to work."

"My turn, my turn!" yelled Zook, nipping past the dragon and placing himself in front of the next Gargantula. Cynder sighed.

"Okay, if you must."

A few squirts of webbing later, and Zook was secreted beneath the Gargantula's body.

"Heh-heh-heh. You gotta try this," came his muffled voice from beneath the spider. "The hairs tickle like crazy. It's brilliant."

The final spider crept toward Cynder, multiple eyes flashing with anticipation.

"Okay, okay, I know. Me next. Just don't get hungry. If those jaws come anywhere near me, it'll be scorched spider, sister."

Cynder was attached to her Gargantula just in time. From her hiding place, she heard the clock strike thirteen, and light blazed all around.

Hurrikazam had arrived.

The Gargantulas immediately scuttled into place at the end of the procession of pies, grabbing the dishes in their jaws.

"Citizens of the Isle of the Undead," the Weather Wizard bellowed from high in the sky. "The Mighty Hurrikazam demands your tribute. Show me the pies!"

"That's our cue," shouted Zook from beneath his spider. "Let's go get him."

Shhh, hissed Cynder. "We don't want him to know we're here."

And then they were moving; the ghost, ghouls and Gargantulas trudging forward obediently, each carrying one of Batterson's tasty pies.

"Mmmmmmm," they heard Hurrikazam say. "They smell even better today. Bring them to MEEEEEE!"

A trembling Morbo watched as the Weather Wizard opened up his vortex and dispatched his tornadoes to collect both pies and pie-bearers.

They whirled down, grabbing the first ghosts and zipping them back up to the cloud.

Cynder heard the shriek of the ghouls that had already been taken. Then she heard Zook calling happily. "He's taken Hex's spider," the Bambazooker babbled. "She's on her way. Me next. Bamboo-yaaaaaaaaaaaaaaaah!"

Zook's cry was lost in the sound of the micro-twister whisking him away. Cynder could feel her Gargantula host trembling in fear and, for a moment, thought the huge spider was going to scuttle off and hide. But then she heard the sound of a tornado roaring toward them and—before she knew what was happening—they were dragged up into the air.

"This is no way to travel," she yelled as they shot upward, spinning around and around and around and around. As she spun, Cynder spotted Morbo raising his top hat in farewell, and, for a split second, she wondered if she'd see him again. Or anything else for that matter.

Chapter Eleven

Into the Cloud

"Getting giiiiiiiddy," Cynder groaned as her whirlwind plunged into Hurrikazam's vortex and spun through what appeared to be a long, winding corridor. She tried to look around, to see where they were being dragged, but it was hopeless. Colors blurred together as they spun and Cynder couldn't tell which way was forward or back, up or down. All she knew for sure was that it felt like they had been traveling for miles.

Then, as suddenly as their dizzying journey began, it came crashing to an end. The tornado simply stopped, and they tumbled down—

Cynder's head still reeling—onto cold stone slabs.

Cynder wanted to call out to her fellow Skylanders, but didn't dare open her mouth. A second later, she was glad she had kept quiet.

"Well, looky here," came a gruff voice from above. Cynder twisted her head to see two heavy-booted feet stomp to a halt beside them. "More Undead losers scooped up by the Wiz. You think you're pretty scary? WRONG!"

There was something really familiar about that voice. Who was it? If only the room would stop spinning.

"Just hear this," the voice continued. "No one better try to escape, or Brock'll show you how to makes things really go bump in the night, savvy?"

Brock! Of course, that's who it was. Brock was a Goliath Drow who had last been seen working with Kaos when Lightning Rod had been trying to find the Air Segment of the Mask of Power. Had he switched allegiances to Hurrikazam now? It certainly made sense. Drow always aligned themselves with whoever was the most powerful, and the Weather Wizard was definitely a force of nature to be reckoned with.

"Follow Brock," the Goliath Drow commanded. "And no funny business."

Cynder lurched from side to side, her nose inches from the floor, as the Gargantulas did as they were told and hurried after Brock.

As they marched, Brock jabbered inanely.

"Hey, cheer up, you guys. The Weather Wizard's Cloud Citadel ain't so bad—unless you're a prisoner and doomed to stay here for all eternity. Oh, like all of you! Hur-hur!"

Cynder promised herself that she would personally fry Brock's backside when she got out of this.

As the procession continued along its way, pungent new smells reached Cynder's nose despite the stink from the giant spiders.

The sweetest smells imaginable, Cynder

said to herself, remembering Rib Cage's words. *There must be flowers everywhere.* She couldn't begin to imagine what the fragrant aroma would be doing to the Undead. It must have been torture.

"And here we are, boys and girls. Final destination."

By the time the procession of captured Island Dwellers reached its destination, the webs securing the Skylanders to the Gargantulas had begun to weaken. Soon they would break altogether, sending the Skylanders tumbling to the floor.

At least the fact that they were loosening gave Cynder the chance to look around the chamber. Brock was herding ghosts, ghouls, and Gargantulas alike on to a long conveyor belt leading to a weird-looking machine at the other end of the room. That must be the gizmo Rib Cage had told them about. A large metallic cloud was suspended above a tall glass tube, pipes and cables snaking up into the high vaulted ceiling. A huge console, covered in all manner of blinking controls and heavy-looking levers, sat behind Brock. As Cynder's Gargantula climbed onto the conveyor belt, she spotted Hex hanging from the belly of her own spider. Cynder could tell that the sorceress was itching to leap from her hiding place. Then again, maybe Hex was just itching due to the scratchy spider hair? Either way, they had to pick the right moment.

Cynder shook her head. Now wasn't the time.

The sound of another voice made Cynder look up.

"So, this is the latest batch, hmmm?"

A small, plump figure had waddled into the chamber, a clipboard tucked under one arm. There was no mistaking who this was, although it had to be said that Hurrikazam's cloud-head had been far more impressive than the real thing.

"Let's get this over and done with," Hurrikazam said, glancing nervously at the trembling Gargantulas. "I can't stand creepy-crawlies. Once found a Fat Belly Spider in my bath. Put me off washing for life."

The little wizard shuffled over to the control console, his extraordinarily long mustache trailing on the floor behind him. He struggled to climb onto the high chair, almost toppling over and landing on his head. He was only saved from cracking his skull by Brock leaping out and grabbing his mustashe.

"I suppose I should say thank you," grumbled Hurrikazam, still dangling by his facial hair. "Now put me back on the chair, you clod-hopping hulk."

"Charmin'," said Brock, tossing the Weather Wizard into the air. The undersized mage flipped head-over-flat-feet and landed with a plop on his surprisingly large bottom. Mumbling something about transforming

Brock into a Snow Drow, Hurrikazam started throwing levers and flicking switches.

The conveyor belt vibrated into life, driving the snatched spirits toward the cloud machine. The spiders started skittering nervously about, especially when the first ghost was deposited in the glass tube beneath the metal cloud.

"Looks like rain," announced the Weather Wizard with little joy. He pulled a large red lever. Immediately water gushed down, drenching the ghost. The spirit wailed an unearthly howl. When the deluge stopped, the figure standing beneath the cloud had changed completely.

It was solid rather than transparent, and it was shivering from the cold. Even stranger still, where it had been bald a minute before, the ex-ghost now sported a huge mop of ginger curls. The entire machine shook as the stolen Undead energy crackled up the pipes to the ceiling.

"What have you done to me?" the former spook moaned.

"Given you a new lease of life," clucked the Weather Wizard. "Now get off the platform. We've got a lot to get through today."

At Brock's signal, two Drow Lance Masters stomped forward and dragged the still-weeping ex-specter from beneath the clouds. The conveyor belt kicked in again, and the next ghost was toppled into the tube with a shriek of panic. This was too much to take for the Gargantula that was carrying Zook. The spider reared up, revealing the Bambazooker hiding beneath, and scuttled off the conveyor belt.

"It's a Skylander!" Brock shouted in alarm, as Zook struggled to pull himself from the webbing. "Think you're here to save the day? WRONG! After him, guys!"

The Drow lurched forward, but Hurrikazam acted first.

"Never fear. There's a cold spell coming!" With a flick of a meaty finger, spider and Bambazooker were both frozen into a huge ice sculpture.

Cynder blasted her webby restraints with spectral lightning. "Volts and lightning, you're going to wish you hadn't done that."

Shooting out from beneath her spider, Cynder lowered her head and charged toward the two Drow, who immediately dropped into a defensive position, spears at the ready.

"Ah, I've never seen the point of those," she quipped as she butted into the first Drow, sending him flying back against the wall. She turned just in time to see the second Lance Master blasted into oblivion by a pair of glowing phantom orbs.

"Fear when I am near," snarled Hex, floating in a blaze of unearthly green light.

"Brock ain't afraid of anyone!" the Goliath Drow roared, charging with fists raised.

"Is that so?" came a muffled voice, accompanied by the sound of cracking ice. Cynder whirled around just in time to see Zook smash out of his frosty prison and slam his own fist into the floor.

"Look out," the Bambazooker yelled triumphantly. "Zook is out!"

Before Brock could stop himself, a wall of barbed cacti burst from the floor between him and Hex. Brock barreled into the vicious spines of the barriers at full pelt.

"Ouch!" he screamed, bouncing back toward Cynder.

"Ouch again!" he squealed as a blast of spectral lightning hit him square in the backside and threw him forward.

"Ouch times three!" he yelped as one of Hex's skulls smacked him straight in the kisser. With a thud, Brock hit the deck hard. He wasn't just seeing stars—he was seeing planets, suns, and even comets.

The Undead Island Dwellers cheered as the Skylanders turned on Hurrikazam, who was trying to hide behind his chair.

"Now to deal with Hurrikaboo-boo," Cynder said, a wicked smile on her lips. "I predict someone is about to be weather-beaten."

"It's about time he learned to fear the dark," Hex added, laughing skulls zipping around her.

"Yeah," Zook agreed, jabbing his bamboo tube toward the Weather Wizard. "I'll teach him to put Zook on ice, too!"

"Don't shoot," Hurrikazam pleaded, shuffling out of his hiding place and raising his hands meekly. "Um, or electrocute me or bombard me with bony heads, for that matter. I'm just very, very glad you're here."

That took Cynder by surprise. "You are?" she asked suspiciously.

"You need to get me out of here." Hurrikazam waddled around the console to meet the Skylanders, almost tripping on his mustache three or four times. "He's holding me prisoner. Making me do the most terrible things!"

"Who is?" asked Zook, equally confused.

Suddenly, the wall behind the console slid up into the ceiling to reveal a whole army of Drow facing them, weapons raised and ready for battle.

"Do you really have to ask?" came a weaselly voice from behind the mass of green warriors. "Is it not obvious?"

Cynder sniffed the air. "Well, now you

come to mention it, I'd recognize that stink anywhere."

"Get out of my way, fools," said the voice as the Drow were jostled around in front of it. "I'm trying to make a dramatic entrance."

A small, bald figure tumbled out of the wall of dark elves, almost tripping over onto his face before righting himself at the last moment.

"That's right, SKYBLUNDERERS," he said, drawing himself up to his completely unimpressive full height. "It is your archfoe. It is KAOOOOOS!"

Chapter Twelve

The Amazing
(Fantastic, Incredible, Surprising, Unfathomable)
All-Colored Rose

Hex's skulls sped up their macabre dance as the sorceress prepared to attack. "We should have known you were behind all this," she said. "Your heart is darker than night itself."

"Oh, stop it," sneered Kaos. "I'll blush. And besides, for a mistress of magic you're obviously terrible at math. I have fifty Drow standing behind me and there are only three of you. Do the math!"

"You're right," agreed Cynder, wings outstretched and ready to fly. "Those odds aren't great . . ."

"Yeah," added Zook, summoning a fungal bloom barrier. "You'll need some more Drow!"

"Leading the charge!" Cynder yelled, and the three Skylanders surged forward.

"Noooooo!" cried out Hurrikazam, lunging forwards and throwing a switch on the control console. Out of nowhere, a tremendous gust of wind sent the Skylanders flying up off the ground. They smashed painfully into the ceiling, the air momentarily driven from their lungs. There they stayed, pressed high against the roof by the force of the gale.

"I thought you wanted our help?" Cynder gasped and gave Hurrikazam her most evil glare. The Weather Wizard slumped against the console and hung his head in shame.

"I do, but if I don't do what he says . . ." Hurrikazam's words failed him and he buried his head in his hands.

"That's right," barked Kaos, almost

jumping up and down with glee. "Let's show the SkyLOSERS what will happen if Hurrikadum-dum defies me. GLUMSHAAAAAANKS!"

Glumshanks, Kaos' loyal and long-suffering troll made his way through the assembled Drow, while the Weather Wizard sobbed in despair. In his hands, Glumshanks was carrying a pot containing the biggest, most vibrant red rose Cynder had ever seen. In fact, to say the flower was red just didn't do its color justice. Even if the word RED was printed in letters one hundred miles high and three hundred miles wide, it still wouldn't describe how red this rose actually was.

And then—BLINK—the rose changed color. The rose wasn't red anymore—it was blue, the bluest blue in the history of blue things. The kind of blue that the sky and the sea and even Lightning Rod could only dream of. The sort of blue that made you forget other colors even existed . . .

Until the rose turned yellow—a yellow so bright that the sun looked dull in comparison. The color of buttercups, daffodils, and fresh custard all rolled together. A shade so cheerful that . . . well, you get the idea.

Let's just say that this was a very special rose.

"Please," the Weather Wizard pleaded, shuffling toward Kaos on his knees. "Not the Amazing, Fantastic, Incredible, Surprising, Unfathomable All-Colored Rose!"

The Portal Master's smirk spread even wider. "What, you mean the Amazing, Fantastic, Incredible, Surprising, Unfathomable All-Colored Rose in this pot here? The only Amazing, Fantastic, Incredible, Surprising, Unfathomable All-Colored Rose in existence? The very same Amazing, Fantastic, Incredible, Surprising, Unfathomable All-Colored Rose that only flowers once every hundred thousand years?" Kaos clicked his fingers and a huge pair of pruning shears appeared in one of his hands.

Chuckling his most evil chuckle, the Portal Master jabbed the shears toward the rose's now-purple flower.

"The Amazing, Fantastic, Incredible, Surprising, Unfathomable All-Colored Rose that I could destroy with a single snip?"

"Yes," wailed the Weather Wizard. "The very same. Please, don't cut it off."

Kaos looked up at the trapped Skylanders. "Now do you see why he does what I tell him?"

"Because of a flower?" Cynder asked, incredulously.

"It is a very pretty flower," admitted Zook.

"And unique," added Hex.

"But is it worth all this?" Cynder asked, not believing her ears. "All the Undead souls he's harvested, all the pain he's caused the Undead, not to mention the chaos all across Skylands. The storm over the Cloudless Desert. That was you, wasn't it? And the freak weather conditions at the Snowcone Mountains and Popcorn Volcano?"

"And don't forget the hailstorms inside the citadel," reminded Zook, trying not to think of Hugo in the bathtub.

"Yes. That was all you, wasn't it?"

Hurrikazam's brow wrinkled in confusion. "What? I don't know what you're talking about."

"Don't worry about all that," shushed Kaos, waving the pruning shears in the air. "All you need to be concerned with is the fact that you are all doomed like you've never been doomed BEFOOOOORE!"

"But why?" Hex asked. "That is what I do not understand."

"Why are you doomed?" The Portal Master snickered. "Because I, KAOS, have you at my mercy, of course!"

"No," continued Hex. "I mean, blackmailing the Undead Island Dwellers, making them un-Undead. What is the purpose?"

"Oh, that." Kaos grinned. "It's simple really. I haven't just been making the

Undead un-Undead. I've been stealing their Undeadishness and storing it up in a huge tank of Undead energy around the back."

"You're stockpiling it," said Cynder, realizing what the Portal Master was saying.

"You're smarter than you look, dragonfly." Kaos chuckled. "And when I have enough I will send clouds to every island in Skylands. Unless I am crowned Emperor of AAAAAAAALL . . ."

"You will shower every island with Undead rain," gasped Cynder.

"Transforming every living soul into a member of the Undead." Hex snarled.

"Wiping out every other Element," completed Zook.

"Oh," said Kaos, looking a smidge disappointed. "That's what I was going to say. But basically, YESSSSSSSSSSSSSSS! You are, I believe the phrase goes, DOOOOOOOOOOOMED!"

Chapter Thirteen

Stormy Weather

Kaos's maniacal laugh lasted for a good five minutes. Even the lines of Drow started checking their watches.

"Um, Master?" piped up Glumshanks, expecting to be clipped around his flapping ears at any moment. "Shouldn't we stop talking about your evil, dastardly plan and actually carry out your evil, dastardly plan before the Skylanders escape and, you know, stop you?"

"WHAAAT?" yelled Kaos, so loudly that Glumshanks took a step back. "Can't an evil genius brag about his work anymore? Oh, very well. WEATHER

WIZAAAAAARD, continue with the Undead EXTRACTIOOOOOON."

Hurrikazam looked at Kaos, then up at the Skylanders, before letting his gaze fall upon the cringing Undead—even the spiders.

"No," he said, quietly, rising to his feet.

"WHAAAAAAT?" screamed Kaos, using twice as many letter A's as before. "Have you forgotten what I'll do if you defy me?"

"No, I haven't," said the Weather Wizard proudly. "But Cynder is right. Yes, the Amazing, Fantastic, Incredible, Surprising, Unfathomable All-Colored Rose may be beautiful; yes, the Amazing, Fantastic, Incredible, Surprising, Unfathomable All-Colored Rose may be the rarest flower in creation; yes, the Amazing, Fantastic, Incredible, Surprising, Unfathomable All-Colored Rose may be my most-prized possession—but these people are worth more than that. You can do what you want, but I won't help you hurt anyone ever again."

"I'll do it!" Kaos threatened, placing

the shear's blades around the rose's fragile stalk. "I'll cut its pretty little head off faster than you can say, 'No, please, spare the Amazing, Fantastic, Incredible, Surprising, Unfathomable All-Colored Rose . . .'"

"Which admittedly would take quite a long time," added Glumshanks.

"I don't care," the Wizard said, jutting his chin out defiantly. "I've done enough storm damage in your name. It stops here and now."

"Go, Wiz!" cheered Zook from up high.

SNIP went Kaos' pruning shears.

"Sob!" went Hurrikazam as the Amazing, Fantastic, Incredible, Surprising, Unfathomable All-Colored Rose's head tumbled from its stalk.

"What's happening?" said Brock, finally waking up.

The Weather Wizard crumbled back to his knees.

In one fluid movement, Kaos leaped forward and grabbed the conveyor belt's controls. The belt hummed back into operation, and the

Undead Island Dwellers began rushing toward the cloud machine.

Kaos flicked another switch, and the conveyor belt got quicker still. "Running at double speed!" Kaos cried in victory as another ghost got drenched by the un-Undeading waters. "Nothing can stop me now. NOTHIIIIING!"

"I don't feel so good," moaned Brock, as two of the Drow rushed over to haul him back to his feet. The hulking Goliath Drow swayed and then tottered forward, throwing out his arms to break his fall. One of his huge, plate-like hands hit a switch.

"NOOOO!" screeched Kaos. "Not that one, IDIOT!"

But the damage was done. The winds that had kept the Skylanders pressed against the ceiling vanished, and they were free. Cynder and Hex swept down majestically—while Zook dropped like a bazooka-wielding stone. Not that plummeting from a great height seemed to faze the Bambazooker. He was firing at the Drow before he had even reached the floor. Upon landing, he bounced straight back up into an attack position.

"Destroy THEEEEEM!" bellowed Kaos, pulling levers expertly. Micro-storms whirled into life all around the Skylanders. Lightning shot toward Cynder, tornadoes surrounded Hex, and Zook was bombarded by a particularly persistent blizzard.

"What is it with these cold snaps?" Zook shivered, still emptying his bazooka into the Drow horde. "Why can't I be attacked by nice weather for a change?"

"Oh, a sun worshipper, are you?" cried out Kaos, pressing a button. "Then catch *these* rays."

A beam of brilliant sunlight blazed down on Zook, knocking him off his feet.

"No . . ." He groaned, his bark instantly cracking in the heat. "Drying up."

Cynder had her own problems. She had

dropped down to protect Hurrikazam and was fighting off the dozens of Drow that were trying to surge forward, while Hex dealt with Brock.

"Can't you use your powers?" Cynder asked Hurrikazam between bolts of spectral lightning. The Weather Wizard shook his head sadly.

"I'm afraid not. I'm not even a real wizard. My machines produce the weather, not me. And by the looks of it, Kaos has mastered the controls."

"I've had plenty of practice," the Portal Master yelled, sending a hailstorm thundering toward Cynder. "While you were tending to your stupid plants, I was taking the Cloud Citadel for a test drive, fool!"

"Stupid plants?" Hurrikazam said, eyes flashing with fury. "You can call me whatever you want, but my plants are NOT STUPID!"

The Weather Wizard twisted his head to the side, and his unfeasibly long mustache

whipped out toward
the control console.
It wrapped around
a lever, and with
another flick of his
head Hurrikazam
pulled it toward him.

BOOM!

The huge door behind
the control console slammed down, trapping
the Drow on the other side. Kaos squeaked in
shock and then dived for cover as Cynder saw
her chance. She spat out a stream of spectral
lightning that danced across the controls.
Sparks flew everywhere as circuits fused
amid the onslaught. All at once, the artificial
weather conditions ceased, and the Skylanders
were free to turn their attentions to Kaos.

"BROCK!" Kaos screamed, looking
everywhere for his Drow bodyguard. "Protect
me. Protect KAOOOOOS!"

"I don't think he's even capable of

protecting himself." Cynder smirked, pointing out the Drow, who was pinned against the wall by seven floating skulls, his eyes rolling wildly in their sockets.

"FOOOL!" shrieked Kaos. "You are officially SACKED!"

"No," wheezed the punch-drunk Drow. "Brock resigns."

"Heh-heh," chuckled Zook, covering Kaos with his bazooka. "Looks like we beat you bad, baldie. Better luck next time."

Kaos pressed himself against the wall, his eyes darting from Zook's blaster to Cynder's grinning jaws.

"Let's not be hasty," he whimpered. "Can't we make a deal?"

"I'd say nice try," Cynder said, rearing up on her back legs, "but it wasn't. You never stood a chance."

She opened her mouth wide, ready to blast Kaos with a no-holds-barred zap of black lightning, when . . .

CRACK! CRACK! CRACK!

Bones burst from the floor around Cynder, trapping her in an ivory prison.

"Woah, what gives?" Another ring of ribs erupted around Zook, knocking his bazooka from his hand. The two bone circles grew and tightened, stretching over the Skylanders' heads so they couldn't escape.

Cynder peered helplessly through the gaps. "Hex?" she asked, eyes wide with disbelief. "What are you doing?"

The sorceress floated between them, never taking her eyes off the cowering Portal Master.

"Saving Kaos," she purred. "What else?"

Chapter Fourteen

Betrayal

"This is not cool!" exclaimed Zook, trying to break the bone bars that encircled him. "Not cool at all!"

"Oh, I don't know," simpered Kaos, a smile returning to his thin lips. "I think things are definitely looking up!"

"Is the machine broken beyond repair?" Hex asked, gliding to stand beside Kaos. When Hurrikazam didn't respond, the sorceress flung out a long, graceful arm. The Wizard shot into the air where he hung, wringing his mustache in fear. "Answer me, fool."

"Ooooh." Kaos giggled. "I usually don't let

other people say 'fool,' but you say it so well."

With a flick of one of Hex's black fingernails, Hurrikazam spun towards the control console.

"N-no," he gabbled, peering over his snotty, hooked nose. "Cynder fused the weather controls, but the Undead Energy Extractor is still operational."

"Hex," Cynder called out from behind the bones. "Let us out of here. We're your friends."

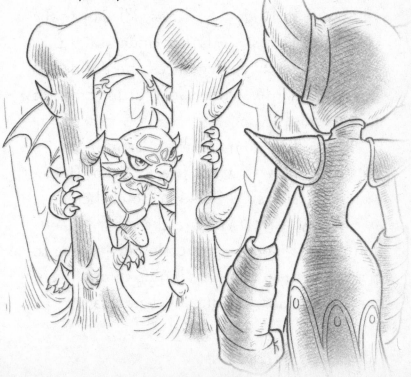

"No," Hex snapped, cutting Cynder dead. "You are not my friends. I haven't had friends since the day I became a member of the Undead. You saw those people on the beach. Even when I saved them, they still feared me. Everyone fears me. I see the way even you look at me when I use my powers. You don't trust me. None of you do. Not even Master Eon."

"That's not true," argued Zook. "You gotta believe us. We're on your side!"

"Talking of sides . . ." Kaos sidled up to the Undead sorceress. "Am I to understand that you have switched allegiances and decided to throw in your lot with Kaos, future Emperor of Skylands?"

Hex spun to face the Portal Master, eyes burning with white fire. "Do not flatter yourself," she spat, looking down her nose at the tiny man. "You are the most hideous individual I have ever had the misfortune to meet. You disgust me. Evil runs through your veins like blood. Your wickedness knows no bounds. Destruction follows you like a shadow. You are hate incarnate."

"And you say the sweetest things." Kaos smirked. "Your point is?"

"You want Undead energy." Hex ignited a glowing orb in her palm. Kaos's eyes grew wide as he stared into its unnatural light. "I am the most powerful Undead sorceress in the history of Skylands. I have more energy than you'd know what to do with."

Cynder's dragon-blood ran cold as she realized what her fellow Undead Skylander was saying.

"Hex! No! You can't do this."

Hex turned and stared Cynder in the eyes.

"I grow tired of being feared." She shifted her attention back to Kaos. "I want to be a normal elf again. Use your machine on me. Wash my Undead powers away."

Chapter Fifteen

Kaos's Finest Hour

It was useless. Cynder blasted her bone prison with wave after wave of spectral lightning, but it wouldn't budge. Zook was the same. He'd tried to dislodge the bones by generating his own rings of blooming bamboo and freaky fungi, but his arboreal assaults shattered as soon as they touched Hex's Undead defences.

Cynder had even tried sending a message back to Master Eon for reinforcements, but the Cloud Citadel blocked her call for help.

Desperately, she summoned an army of exploding ghosts, but they didn't even scratch her bone prison's surface. Here, in a part of Skylands already brimming with Undead energy, Hex's magic was just too strong— and soon all that power would belong to Kaos.

Hex had just watched as the last of the Undead were processed by the Weather Wizard's cloud machine. Even the Gargantulas had been shrunk down to the size of helpless money spiders. And now it was her own turn.

"You don't have to do this!" Cynder cried out as Hex took her place beneath the metallic cloud. "There must be another way!"

Hex wouldn't even look at her former friend now. She simply shook her head. "No," she whispered, sadly. "There is not."

"Are you ready, my dear?" Kaos cooed, batting his eyelids from behind the control panel. Glumshanks stood beside his master, clutching Hurrikazam's clipboard, the traitorous Weather Wizard having been tied to the chair by his own mustache.

Hex nodded. "Yes. Do it now, before I change my mind."

"Gladly," Kaos smirked and pulled the big red lever.

The metallic cloud thundered and the rain started to fall.

"No!" Cynder cried out, slashing at the bones with her claws, trying to cut her way through to Hex. She wanted to dive in and pull the sorceress free before it was too late. This could not be happening.

The cloud machine sparked with dark unearthly energies.

"Look at these readings, Glumshanks," Kaos cried out, clapping his hands together. "Such power, and it's all mine, MINE, MIIIIIIIINE!"

But the little troll was beginning to look worried. "You're right, Lord Kaos. It is a lot of power."

"More than I ever dreamed we'd collect. More than even the Mask of Power would have granted me. I will be UNSTOPPABLE!"

"Do you think it is too much power?" Glumshanks asked.

"Too much power?" Kaos laughed. "That's a good one. There's no such thing as too much power, my foolish fool."

Cynder's ears pricked up as Glumshanks continued to worry aloud. "There is if the machine gets overloaded!"

"What?" snapped Kaos, stopping his cackling immediately. A warning light started to flash on the console.

Glumshanks was frantically throwing switches and yanking levers. "The Undead batteries are full."

A second light began to flash.

"The generators are at full capacity."

Half a dozen lights began to flash and, obviously feeling left out, a warning siren began to wail.

"The entire grid is going to blow!" Glumshanks yelled.

"Turn it off," commanded Kaos in complete and utter panic. "Turn it off!"

"You can't!" realized Cynder, and turned back to the Cloud Machine. "That's what Hex was planning all along."

Zook had also figured out what was happening. "She wasn't lying when she said she was the most powerful Undead sorceress in Skylands—more powerful than your machine can handle."

"She's going to blow it sky-high!" shouted Hurrikazam, laughing despite his predicament.

"Never!" Kaos shrieked, lunging across the console for the door control. Behind the Skylanders, the wall slid back into the ceiling to reveal Kaos's Drow minions—most of them still singed from Cynder's earlier attacks.

"What are you waiting for, fools?" Kaos demanded, pointing towards the cloud machine. "Get that witch out of the rain!"

The Drow forces surged forward as one,

barging past the bone prisons, before pausing in front of the Undead Energy Extractor. The metallic cloud was glowing white hot and the torrent of rain was a bright luminous green.

"Lord Kaos, it's going to explode," Glumshanks yelled, pulling on his Master's sleeve. "Get down!"

Sure enough, with a *boom* that sounded like the universe itself being torn in two, the cloud machine erupted into brilliant emerald flames.

Chapter Sixteen

The Final Battle

If you've ever wondered what the universe being torn in two actually sounds like, then imagine the shriek of a metal sheet being ripped down the middle. Add to that the sound of a brick wall being demolished, half a dozen pianos being dropped to the ground from the moon, a million elephants blowing their noses, and every cymbal in the galaxy being crashed at the same time. The resulting cacophony would seem like a mouse's whisper compared to the noise the Cloud Machine made when it went *bang*. Even Sonic Boom would have struggled to be heard above it.

The good news is that the shockwave not only shattered the Skylanders' bone prisons but also sent the Drow smashing into the walls.

Cynder had covered her ears seconds before the machine had blown up, while Zook had crammed mushrooms into his lug-holes just in time. They ran over to the broken glass tube where the Cloud Machine had once stood and paused nervously in front of the slumped figure at its feet with its back to them.

"Hex?" Cynder ventured, reaching out with a claw and then thinking better of it.

"Can you hear us?" Zook asked.

The figure in black stirred and turned to face them. Cynder gasped. It was Hex's face, but her skin wasn't its usual deathly pale. It was green, her cheeks flushed dark emerald. Her eyes, which were usually white, were now dark, dancing with life.

"Why are you looking at me like that?" she asked, her voice softer than it had ever sounded.

"You're no longer Undead," said Zook in awe. "The machine cured you."

Hex looked at her green fingers, seeing them that way for the first time in hundreds of years.

Cynder felt a lump in her throat. "It's what you've always wanted, Hex."

Hex raised an eyebrow and looked at her friend with an amused expression. "You are joking, aren't you?" She closed her eyes and muttered a secret spell. The other Skylanders gazed as the sorceress floated into the air, arms raised. Energy crackled around her hands as her fingers became blue once more. The color crept across her hands, up her arms, and over to her neck before covering her whole face. When she opened her eyes, they were blazing white. "Nothing more than a lingering effect of the Undead Energy Extractor. This is who I am, and this is the way I want to be. I embrace my dark side. I always have."

"Woo!" Zook cheered, punching the air. "That's our Hexy, right there."

"And not a moment too soon," said Cynder, looking over her shoulder. "We've got company."

Zook turned to see what remained of Kaos's Drow army creeping towards them, lances at the ready.

"These guys never give up," the Bambazooker complained, although he sounded anything but disappointed.

"We do not stand alone against the forces of Darkness," Hex announced, summoning a storm of skulls. "Behold. As my power was returned to me, so is theirs."

The Lance Master at the front of the legion looked puzzled at Hex's words, but was soon distracted as a money spider crawled across his nose. He was even more distracted when the money spider transformed into a hungry, hairy Gargantula.

All around, the un-Undeaded Undead became Undead again and joined the fight with gusto.

"Heh-heh. Good to have you back!" shouted Zook to Hex while pumping mushroom mortars into the dark Drow hordes.

"I never went away. Oh, and if you call me Hexy again"—Hex smiled, blasting a Drow Archer with an enchanted troll skull—"I'll turn you into a toad!"

It made Cynder smile to hear her friends joking with each other. This was more like it. The Drow didn't stand a chance.

Then, out of the corner of her eye, she noticed the Weather Wizard desperately trying to get her attention.

"Skylander," Hurrikazam cried out, still bound by his own mustache. "It's Kaos!"

Cynder glanced around. The Portal Master had gone.

"Where is that creep?"

"He's heading for my botanical gardens, where I grow my plants. Oh, the damage he could do. For a start there's my Slime-encrusted Geranium. And my Lesser-spotted Pig Orchid. And . . ."

Cynder didn't wait to hear the rest of the list. Checking that the other Skylanders could handle the Drow, she sped out of the control chamber.

* * *

"Where is it?" Kaos was screaming when Cynder found him, upending flowerpots beneath an old oak tree. "WHERE?"

Glumshanks gulped when he noticed Cynder watching them, and tapped his master on the shoulder.

"Um, Lord Kaos. We have company . . ."

Kaos span round, his red eyes widening when he saw Cynder.

"Oh, it's the little dragonfly. Am I supposed to be scared?"

"Yes," admitted Glumshanks glumly, receiving a sharp elbow in the ribs from Kaos.

"What are you looking for, Kaos?" Cynder asked, taking a step forward. "An escape route? I'm shocked."

"Shocked? Ha-ha-ha-HAAAA!" the Portal Master laughed, throwing his arms wide. "You will be. Summon my Fearsome Flock of Flying Flowerpots . . ."

"Your what?" Cynder sniggered. "And *that's* suppose to scare me?"

"You have to admit, flowerpots aren't that scary . . . ," pointed out Glumshanks, scratching his ear absently.

"Really?" Kaos asked, biting his lip. "Hmmmm. Okay, how about this? Summon my Fearsome Flock of Flying Flowerpots OF DOOOOOOOM!"

"Better." Glumshanks nodded.

All at once, every flowerpot around the gardens rose into the air and flung themselves at Cynder. She leaped back, smashing them in midair with her spectral lightning. The only problem was that for every flowerpot that she destroyed, three more were ready to beat her senseless.

"Now, Glumshanks," she heard Kaos say, "let's find the seed and go."

There was nothing Cynder could do. If she stopped firing at the flowerpots, she would be battered.

And then she noticed something. A large

oak tree was starting to transform. Its branches were becoming arms, a face appearing on its trunk. It was Dogwood the Stump Demon! Or at least it would be by the time it had become truly Undead again.

"Kaos," she cried out between blasts. "If you're looking for the Weather Wizard's special seed, I definitely didn't see it beneath that old tree."

Kaos's head snapped around.

"What's that, Skyblunderer?"

"I said there's no point searching beside that old oak tree. It won't be there."

The Portal Master threw back his head and laughed. "Ha! Do you really think I, KAOS, would fall for such a transparent ploy?"

Well, it was worth a shot, thought Cynder as she dodged a particularly large low-flying flowerpot.

"If you're saying the seed isn't beneath the tree, then it obviously is! You have to get up early to trick Kaos! Come on, Glumshanks."

Cynder grinned. *Gotcha!*

"Um, Lord Kaos," mumbled Glumshanks. "You know, I think this might actually be a trick."

"Nonsense," shrieked Kaos, rushing over to the tree. "The seed is here. I can feel it. No one makes a fool of . . ."

"KAOS!" growled Dogwood, his transformation complete.

"Whoops!" said Kaos as the Stump Demon grabbed both Portal Master and gangly troll in his strong wooden arms.

Cynder smashed the last of the flowerpots and stalked toward the Stump Demon.

"Have you met my friend, Dogwood?" she asked slyly. "Don't worry, his bark is worse than his bite." She paused, considering this. "Or is it the other way around?"

"Let go of me!" Kaos screamed. "I am Kaos, I am . . ."

"Well and truly beaten?" asked Zook, running up behind Cynder. "As are your Drow, by the way. Heh-heh!"

"They took a walk on the dark side," Hex confirmed, appearing beside them.

"Do you really think my plans have been foiled, FOOLS?" screamed Kaos.

"Yes," said Glumshanks.

"Not you!" snapped the Portal Master, before turning his attention to the Skylanders again. "Okay, so my plans have been foiled, but there will be other plans. Oh yes. Unstoppable plans. Unstoppable plans that will never be stopped. Unstoppable plans that will . . ."

"Oh, just summon a Portal and escape back to your lair, already," Cynder said, rolling her eyes and sighing.

Kaos's face fell. "You people have no sense of melodrama!" he moaned, snapping his fingers. There was a flash of light, and Kaos and Glumshanks were gone.

Chapter Seventeen

An Unexpected Offer

"What a terrible day!" cheered Mayor Morbo when the Skylanders returned from the Cloud Citadel, every Undead Island Dweller safely returned—including a very grateful Flunky. "Truly horrendous!"

"I'd thought he'd be pleased," said Zook.

"He is!" laughed Cynder. "Remember?"

"Heh! I'll never get the hang of Undead talk," admitted Zook with a grin.

Hex swept towards the mayor. "And we have brought others with us. Others who want to apologize."

She moved aside to reveal Hurrikazam and

a bashful looking Brock. The hulking Drow was the first to shuffle forward.

"Um, Brock, sorry. Brock just wanted to make Master happy. Oh, and the pies. Brock an idiot!"

"No, Brock," Hurrikazam said softly, stepping towards the Night Mayor. "I'm the biggest idiot of them all. I am truly sorry for what I have done to you and your people. I do not deserve your forgiveness, but I promise you this. I will build you your own Weather Machine so you can be sure of dark and stormy nights all year round."

Morbo rattled his chains in delight. "How hateful. I despise it! Thank you, Weather Wizard. You will always be unwelcome here on the Isle of the Undead."

The mayor turned toward Hex.

"As will you, sorceress."

The Undead Skylander looked shocked.

"Really?"

"Of course. We would be honored if you came to live here, where you belong."

Cynder frowned. Surely Hex wouldn't stay? Not after everything they'd been through.

"Thank you, Mayor," Hex said softly, with real warmth in her cold voice. "But I already belong somewhere. With my friends. The Skylanders."

"Heh-heh! You sure do." Zook chuckled.

"What about you, my boy?" Hurrikazam asked Brock. "Where will you go now?"

The Goliath Drow shrugged his broad shoulders. "Brock hasn't a clue."

The Weather Wizard started searching his robes for something. "Have you ever heard of Rumbletown?" he said, pulling out a small velvet bag. "I think you'd like it. They love a good scrap there. And there are plenty of pie shops. I could drop you off?"

As Brock beamed, Hurrikazam turned to Cynder. "And I have something for you, my dear. Hold out your paw."

Cynder did what she was told for once, and the Weather Wizard tipped a small yellow seed into her palm.

"What is it?" she asked, peering at the seed.

"The only Amazing, Fantastic, Incredible, Surprising, Unfathomable All-Colored Rose seed in existence," Hurrikazam said sadly. "Thanks to Kaos."

"But why give it to us?" Hex asked.

"Because it's so much more," the Weather Wizard smiled. "A seed bursting with life, with potential, the complete opposite of the Undead Element. Take it to Master Eon. He's been looking for it."

"Hey, hey, hey," said Zook. "You're not saying what I think you're saying?"

Hurrikazam nodded.

"It's the Undead segment." Cynder gasped in awe.

"Of the Mask of Power, yes," Hurrikazam confirmed. "Kaos knew I had it, but I wouldn't tell him where for obvious reasons. Take care of it."

"We will," promised Cynder. "Thank you."

"We should transport the segment back to the archive immediately," insisted Hex, placing a finger on her temple. "I shall call for

Master Eon to send a Portal." The sorceress paused. "Hmmm. That's strange."

"What is?" asked Zook.

"I can't reach Master Eon. He's not answering."

Cynder felt a shiver run down her tail. "That's bad. And not in an Undead way."

"Don't worry," said Hurrikazam, pulling a control out of his pocket. "I have a portable weather machine here. I can summon a storm to blow you all the way back to the Eternal Archive." He flicked a switch, and three tornadoes spun into life above them. "Hop on!" he grinned.

"Here we go again." Zook laughed and jumped into one of the twisters.

By the time Hurrikazam's tornadoes dropped the three Skylanders outside the Eternal Archive, Spyro was already running up to greet them, with Hugo scampering behind.

"Thank the Benevolent Ancients you have returned," blustered Hugo.

"Hey, hey, hey, little fella. What's happened?" asked Zook.

"Squirmgrub has vanished," Hugo replied, "Completely disappeared."

Cynder couldn't pretend to be upset. "Well, good riddance, I say. I've never trusted him."

"You'll trust him even less now," Spyro added, his face grave.

"Master Eon!" Hex said. "Has something happened to him?"

Spyro nodded. "Wherever Squirmgrub has gone, he's taken Master Eon with him. Master Eon has been kidnapped!"

SKYLANDERS UNIVERSE

THE MASK OF POWER
STUMP SMASH
CROSSES THE
BONE DRAGON

Chapter One

Missing!

Stump Smash was having a bad day. All the Skylanders were. A day they thought would never happen. Could never happen.

Master Eon had disappeared.

No, it was more serious than that. Master Eon had been kidnapped, spirited away by agents of Kaos, their archenemy and the most wicked soul Skylands had ever produced. The Skylanders had no idea where Master Eon had been taken. They weren't even sure how—although they had some very nasty suspicions.

As he stomped through the echoing corridors of the Eternal Archive, Stump Smash played through recent events in his mind. The Skylanders had been searching for the eight Elemental fragments of an ancient weapon known as the Mask of Power. They were still a bit confused about what the Mask of Power actually did, although legend suggested it made its wearer all-powerful. Kaos was also searching for the fragments, and had managed to get his evil little hands on the Tech segment already. Fortunately, the Skylanders had beaten him to four of the other fragments, guided by the Book of Power and Other Utterly Terrifying Stuff (Vol. 3).

The book was held right here in the Eternal Archive. Or at least it used to be.

The book had gone missing, along with Master Eon. Only a Portal Master could read its pages. A Portal Master like Eon or Kaos.

At least Kaos hadn't managed to reach the fragments that the Skylanders had already collected, thought Stump Smash as he strode through the archive's vast vaults. The Water, Air, Earth, and Undead segments were safely locked away. Nothing could get them.

"What do you mean, Kaos got to them?" Stump heard Spyro the dragon splutter as he rounded a corner.

Spyro was standing open-mouthed, staring at a large robotic figure in disbelief. Chief Curator Wiggleworth was a Warrior Librarian, the protector of thousands of powerful books here in the Archive. Like all Warrior Librarians, he was an imposing figure, towering over Spyro in a suit of gleaming mechanical armor. At the heart of the suit squirmed Wiggleworth's true form, a tiny and incredibly old bookworm who was also one of Master Eon's most trusted friends.

"I don't know what's happened," Wiggleworth said. "No one should have been able to open the vault but Squirmgrub and I—"

"Squirmgrub." Stump Smash rumbled, interrupting the conversation. "The Warrior Librarian you assigned to help us guard the fragments."

Wiggleworth's mechanical head drooped. Squirmgrub had been one of the curator's most trusted librarians, until he was revealed to be an agent of Kaos himself. He had spirited Master Eon away to goodness knows where and stolen the fragments of the Mask for his dark master.

"He was a traitor," Spyro growled. "A double-agent."

Stump Smash had never seen Spyro look so angry. The purple dragon was many things. Adventurous, yes. Impulsive, definitely. But he always kept his temper in check. Unlike Stump himself.

This time was different. Spyro's red eyes were burning with rage.

"Don't you see, Wiggleworth?" Spyro said. "This means Kaos now has five of the eight fragments." The dragon turned toward the open safe door. "We should never have stored them here. We should have taken them to Eon's citadel. They would have been safe there."

The Curator shrugged, mechanical shoulders whirring. "But Master Eon said . . ."

"Master Eon is gone," Spyro snapped, whirling around. "Because of you!"

Stump Smash raised his mallet fists, trying to calm the situation. "Spyro, this isn't helping . . ."

The dragon turned on the Life Skylander. "But we let him down, Stump. We let Master Eon get captured."

"We didn't even know he was in danger," Stump insisted.

"We should have! We're Skylanders. We protect Skylands. That's what we do!"

"That's what we were doing," Stump reminded him. "We were busy and Kaos struck—but we'll find Master Eon. I promise."

Spyro took a deep breath, his raised scales relaxing slightly. "I know," he said finally, nodding. "Have we heard from the others?"

Stump Smash wished he was bringing good news. He shook his trunk. "Lightning Rod and Zoo Lou are searching Fantasm Forest. Scratch and Flashwing are on their way to Molekin Mine."

Spyro sighed. "It's taking so long without being able to use Portals."

"Yes," muttered Wiggleworth. "Well, we can't use them without . . ."

His voice trailed away as Spyro shot him a look. "Without a Portal Master," the dragon said in a voice that was frostier than an ice-clops's snowcone. "Yes, we know."

Another voice echoed around the chamber. "Spyro, where are you?"

It was Flameslinger, a Fire Skylander and one of Stump Smash's oldest friends.

"Over here, Sling," the powerful tree called out.

Flameslinger tore around the corner, skidding to a halt in front of them, a red hot trail sizzling in his wake. The elf was always on the move, rushing here, there and everywhere. He wasn't one for cooling his heels. Behind him, a smaller, dumpier figure struggled to keep up. This was Hugo, Master Eon's right-hand Mabu. The little fellow was a natural panicker, but he had impressed Stump Smash since Master Eon had vanished. Stump had expected the Mabu to fall to pieces, but Hugo was rising to the challenge, helping to coordinate the search for the missing Portal Master.

"We've got a problem." Hugo wheezed, huffing and puffing as he joined the others. "I mean, another one."

"I'm not going to like this, am I?" said Spyro with a sigh, sharing a look with Stump Smash.

"Well, you told us to listen out for

anything weird," said Flameslinger. "And this sounds pretty weird to me."

"What does?" asked Stump Smash.

"It's the Giggling Forest," Hugo replied, peering over his oversize glasses. "Spyro, it's started to cry."

Chapter Two

The Weeping Forest

"Okay, run this by me again," said Flynn. "There's a forest that laughs?"

"We've explained twice already," Flameslinger snapped, holding on to the edge of the hot-air balloon's jiggling basket.

"Hey, hot stuff," grinned Flynn, the pilot, pulling a lever and trying to ignore the fact that it came off in his hand. "I've been kinda busy here, trying not to crash."

"That's a first," grumbled Flameslinger under his breath.

Stump Smash understood the elf's frustration. As soon as Spyro had heard about the Giggling Forest, he had dispatched Stump and Flameslinger to investigate, along with Tech Skylander Countdown and Magic Skylander Wrecking Ball. They'd called upon Flynn to transport them to the forest in his hot-air balloon. Flynn was Skylands' best pilot. They knew this because Flynn was always telling them. He'd pointed it out three times before they'd even taken off, and twice since nearly smashing the basket into the Eternal Archive's tallest turret. The Mabu was almost as full of hot air as one of his balloons, but he'd helped them many times over the years. There was a good heart beating in that puffed-up chest.

"The clue's in the name, Flynn," Stump said. "The Giggling Forest giggles. All the time. Has done for thousands of years."

"What's the joke?" Flynn asked, spinning the wheel to narrowly avoid a school of sky-salmon, only to find himself heading straight for a flying whale.

"No one knows," Stump replied, stumbling into Wrecking Ball, who had wrapped his tongue around the ropes to stop himself being flung from the basket. "Guess they're just happy."

"Not any more," pointed out Countdown. "What's-his-name said they'd started crying."

"Flameslinger!" The elf laughed, before shrugging at Flynn. "Don't mind Countdown, he gets forgetful."

"Do I?" asked Countdown. "Can't remember."

Wrecking Ball snickered but couldn't join in the conversation. He was a little tongue-tied, after all.

"This isn't good," said Countdown. "This isn't good, at all."

They were standing in the middle of a clearing in the Giggling Forest, after making what some would call a bumpy landing. Flynn was calling it awesome, but he was also trying to rebuild the basket that had "accidentally" smashed into the ground. The pilot also claimed that someone must have raised the island by a few yards at the last minute, but the Skylanders were too taken aback by the sound greeting them to argue.

The trees of the Giggling Forest weren't just crying. They were wailing.

"Stump, you better talk to them," said Wrecking Ball.

"Why me?" asked Stump Smash.

"Because you're a tree?" suggested Flameslinger.

Stump Smash couldn't argue with that. He marched forward to the nearest blubbing trunk.

"Hey, what's up?" he asked, trying to get the tree's attention. "Feeling a little blue?"

The tree stopped sniffling for a second, looked at Stump with watery eyes, and then bawled. "We're so sad," it howled, sap streaming from its wooden nose.

"We kinda noticed," said Countdown, walking up beside the Life Skylander. "But what gives?"

"You better see for yourselves," the tree sniffed, waving them farther into the forest with a trembling branch. "It's awful."

Why is the Giggling Forest so sad? Where has Squirmgrub taken Master Eon? And can the Skylanders retrieve the stolen segments of the Mask of Power before it's too late?

Find out in . . .

STUMP SMASH
CROSSES THE BONE DRAGON